CASE FILES

NOTES, STATS, AND FACTS FROM

DETECTIVE PIKACHU

by Meredith Rusu

Scholastic Inc.

ISBN 978-1-338-52944-9

10 9 8 7 6 5 4 3 2 1   19 20 21 22 23

Cover design by Katie Fitch

Interior design by Cheung Tai

Printed in the U.S.A.   40

First printing 2019

CONTENTS

INTRODUCTION

Hey there, kid. Nice to meet you. Welcome to the world of **DETECTIVE PIKACHU**: expert crime solver. He may not be what you'd typically expect a world-class detective to look like—for one thing, he's just a little over a foot tall. So if chasing clues takes a normal guy ten steps, it takes him a thousand. For another thing, most people can't understand him. All they hear is, *"Pika, pika!"* (Adorable? Yes. Helpful during an interrogation? Not really.)

But not you. Because you're special. You're reading this book filled with his master case files, and that means you've got the *fire* in you. The *super-sleuth* fire. That burning desire, hot as a Charizard's flame, to tackle any mystery head-on and crack the case.

And boy, has he got a whopper of a case this time. And he's not going to rest until he's figured out the truth behind what happened. Even if he has to travel across the land, searching far and wide, in order to understand the power that's . . . huh, that sounds vaguely familiar. Weird.

So, what do you say? Are you up for a little gumshoe sleuthing? Don't worry—Detective Pikachu will start from the beginning and help you to follow the tracks and dig up clues. By the time you've reached the end of this book, you'll have all the info you need in order to solve this mystery. Or, at least you'll have all the info that Detective Pikachu has right now. But as long as you're working together, you'll be calling this case closed faster than a Thunderbolt attack. After all, you're dealing with a world-class detective. And that's a cold, hard fact.

THE FACTS

From Detective Pikachu's Case Files

Let's start from the beginning. Everything first went down in Ryme City. This place is like nothing you've ever seen before, because it's a city where humans and Pokémon live and work together side by side.

Ryme City:
A Harmonious Masterpiece

Throughout history, Pokémon have been part of our world. Early humans used to catch them and train them to use their unique powers for the common good. This relationship evolved into what we now refer to as Pokémon battles.

But then came Ryme City: a remarkable place where humans and Pokémon can live side by side and humans and Pokémon work together. There's simply . . . harmony.

Howard Clifford created Ryme City years ago. He also owns Clifford News Media (CNM). And he has an adult son, Roger Clifford.

WELCOME TO RYME CITY

WHERE PEOPLE AND POKÉMON COEXIST

RYME CITY COUNCIL

INTRODUCTION

Some of Harry's many awards for his police work.

It was in Ryme City that Detective Pikachu partnered with Harry Goodman, one of the greatest detectives in the area.

But now, Harry is missing. What happened to him? Detective Pikachu is determined to find out.

FIERY CRASH ON THE EDG

"I KNOW YOU CAN'T UNDERSTAND ME. BUT PUT DOWN THE STAPLER, OR I . . . WILL ELECTROCUTE . . . YOU."

THE LINEUP

Now that you know the basic facts, it's time to bring in the lineup. These are the people that Detective Pikachu has met along the way in his case-cracking quest. Some of them are helpful . . . some of them not so much. And some are just plain weird. But dealing with all different types comes along with the job description.

How well do any of us really know anyone?

TIM GOODMAN

Tim is Harry Goodman's son. Tim hadn't seen his dad in a while, but recently discovered he is missing. Now he wants to find his father.

Tim Goodman Facts

- Son of Harry Goodman
- Works as an insurance agent
- Dreamed of being a Pokémon Trainer as a kid
- Has a rocky relationship with his dad

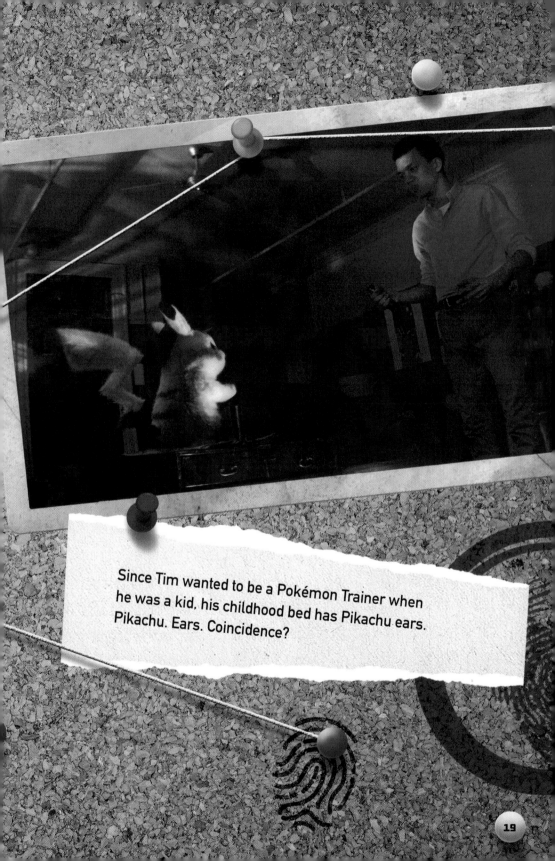

Since Tim wanted to be a Pokémon Trainer when he was a kid, his childhood bed has Pikachu ears. Pikachu. Ears. Coincidence?

THE LINEUP

To his surprise, Tim discovered Detective Pikachu in Harry's apartment. And to his even greater surprise, Tim can understand Detective Pikachu. Instead of just hearing, *"Pika! Pika!"* Tim can hear him speaking in words!

Neither of them can explain it. Can any other humans understand any other Pokémon?

Tim and Detective Pikachu decided to work together. After all, they're both looking for Harry.

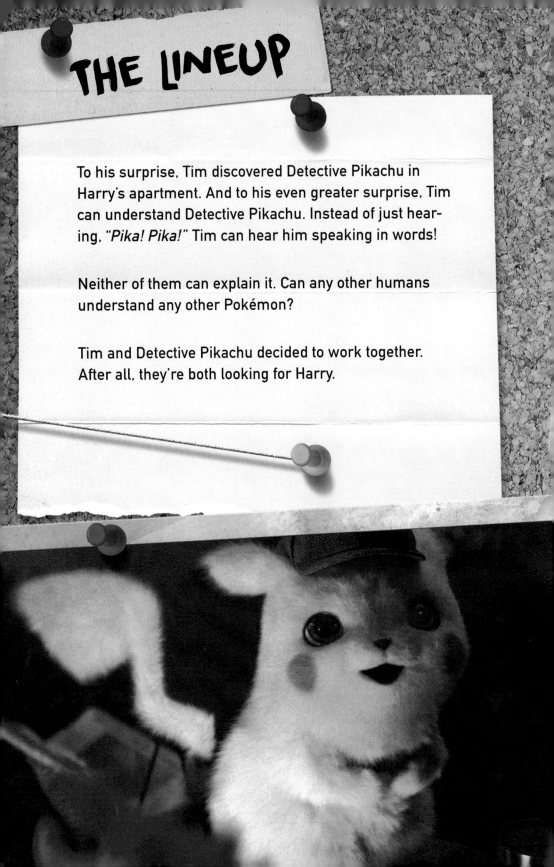

It's unclear who was more surprised when Tim could understand Detective Pikachu's speech.

LUCY STEVENS

Detective Pikachu and Tim met Lucy during their investigation, and she joined them on the way.

Psyduck has mysterious psychic powers that it can't always control!

Lucy Stevens Facts

- Young and ambitious
- Eager to sniff out a story
- Has a Psyduck for a Pokémon partner

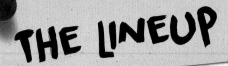

LIEUTENANT HIDE YOSHIDA

Hide Yoshida is a lieutenant at the Ryme City Police Department, and used to work with Harry Goodman. Could he have been involved in Harry's disappearance? Tim and Detective Pikachu don't really think so—when they met Lieutenant Yoshida, they couldn't help but like him. But you never know . . .

Lieutenant Yoshida Facts

- Police lieutenant in Ryme City

- Good friend of Harry Goodman

- Honorable guy (as far as we know)

Lieutenant Yoshida had nothing but nice things to say about working with Harry Goodman.

"THERE'S MAGIC THAT BROUGHT US TOGETHER. AND THAT MAGIC IS CALLED HOPE."

THE LOCATION LOWDOWN

Okay. You've got the who's who. Now you need to know the what's where. So listen up: here are the deets on the digs—all the haunts where you'll hunt for clues with Tim and Detective Pikachu. Just remember to stick close to them. You don't want to go wandering into something dangerous.

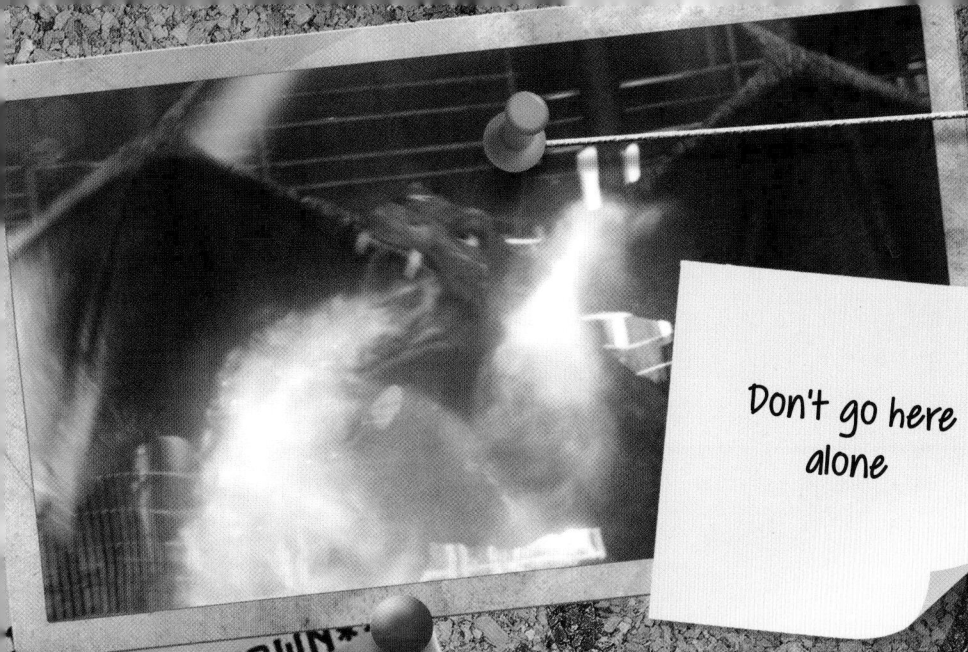

Don't go here alone

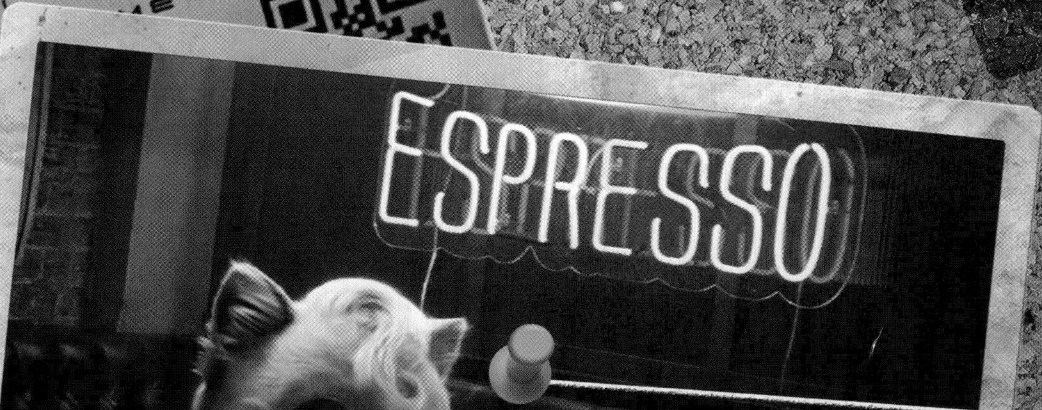

Best cup of coffee in town

DONT WALK

WALK
PUSH BUTTON TO CROSS

Detective Pikachu by a food vendor

RYME CITY

This mecca of human/Pokémon coexistence has pretty much anything a human or Pokémon could ever want. During the day, citizens flood the streets heading to work, play, eat—you name it. At night, the downtown marketplace lights up with food stands and street vendors.

The Ryme City business district stays pretty clean, but the docks are another story. Sketchy characters dipping in and out of the shadows there is so common, it's borderline cliché, and if you're smart, you don't hang around after dark. Unless you're looking for trouble . . . or clues.

NO ENTRY
AUTHORIZED
PERSONNEL
ONLY

LCOME TO
ME CITY

WHERE PEOPLE
POKÉMON COEXIST

RYME CITY COUNCIL

THE HI-HAT CAFÉ

This hole-in-the-wall café is just no-frills enough to be a local dive, but it's also frequented enough that you can eavesdrop on conversations around you to hear the word on the street. Learn to lay low, listen hard, and sip your coffee slowly, and you're sure to pick up any intel you need.

Detective Pikachu *loves* coffee, and wants it all the time—he's sure that it helps him get into the right mental state for solving mysteries. So the Hi-Hat Café is basically heaven for him.

Detective Pikachu's coffee order: black as night, and with an extra shot.

You never know who you might find at the café.

HARRY GOODMAN'S APARTMENT

Detective Pikachu and Tim first met at Harry's apartment in Ryme City. They were not expecting to find each other there! But after they got to know each other, it gave them a good place to start looking for clues.

Harry's desk. Did he leave anything for Tim and Detective Pikachu to find?

THE POLICE PRECINCT

Since Harry was a detective and worked at the police precinct, Tim and Detective Pikachu ended up back there to get whatever intel they could.

Detective Pikachu's Tips

1) Detective work means not always operating according to plan.

2) It means dealing with things in the moment.

FIGHTING ARENA

Going to this seedy battleground alone is not recommended.
And you especially don't want to find yourself in the ring . . .

"IF YOU WANT TO FIND YOUR POPS, I'M YOUR BEST BET."

DETECTIVE PIKACHU

WELCOME TO

RYME CITY

WHERE PEOPLE
AND POKÉMON COEXIST

RYM
ROADSID
&
24/7 T

uel d

O ENTRY

AUTHORIZED
PERSONNEL
ONLY

THE CASE SO FAR . . .

All right, gumshoe. You've been brought up to speed on where the case stands.

Detective Pikachu, Tim, and Lucy are on the hunt, and you're joining them. Hold on to your deerstalker cap! Things are going to get *detective-y*. It's time to go through Pokémon one by one to gather as many clues as possible, to track down the answer to the ultimate mystery: *What happened to Harry Goodman?*

—MISSING

PSYDUCK

—MISSI

CHARIZA

—MISSING

B LBASAU

=SING=

=MISSING=

LOUDRED

=G=

=MISSING=

=MISSING=

ESPRESSO

LUDICOLO

JIGGLYPUFF

AIPOM

Aipom are Pokémon that are so nimble with their tails and do so much with them that their hands have started to become clumsy from lack of use.

AIPOM FACTS

- Normal-type Pokémon
- Height: 2'07"
- Weight: 24.5 lbs.
- Evolves into Ambipom

Involved with Harry's Disappearance?

Not sure. These guys can really climb around, so they could be involved in anything.

MISSING

AIPOM

MISSING

ARCANINE

ARCANINE

Arcanine are known for their high speed. There are so many amazing tales from history about Arcanine that you'd think they were actually legendary . . . but, really, you see them all over the place.

ARCANINE FACTS

- Fire-type Pokémon
- Height: 6'03"
- Weight: 341.7 lbs.
- Evolved form of Growlithe

Involved with Harry's Disappearance?

Do you think Arcanine knows anything? Think quickly, before it makes a speedy getaway!

MISSING

BULBASAUR

BULBASAUR

Bulbasaur likes to nap in the sunshine, and while it sleeps, the seed on its back catches the rays and uses the energy to grow. Man, are these guys connected to nature, or what?

BULBASAUR FACTS

- Grass- and Poison-type Pokémon
- Height: 2'04"
- Weight: 15.2 lbs.
- Evolves into Ivysaur

Involved with Harry's Disappearance?

Bulbasaur don't seem to be related to it . . . but you never know.

CHARIZARD

Unlike Charmander, Charizard has a near-constant chip on its shoulder. It's known to rebuke its own Trainers in battle, and it really just cares about finding the strongest opponent to face. The more it battles, the hotter its flame breath grows.

CHARIZARD FACTS

- Fire- and Flying-type Pokémon
- Height: 5'07"
- Weight: 199.5 lbs.

Involved with Harry's Disappearance?

This Pokémon has a bone to pick with anyone who crosses its path. If Harry got in its way, there's a possibility Charizard tried to help snuff him out.

MISSING

CHARIZARD

JIGGLYPUFF

You know how sometimes you see a performer, and you just *know* that one day they're going to be a star? Well, Jigglypuff is *not* that star. But no one gave Jigglypuff the memo, because it insists on performing its soothing lullaby (consisting of one lyric: its name) to anyone who will listen. And a lot of people who don't want to listen, too. Inevitably, the song lulls people to sleep, and that makes Jigglypuff turn into a bit of a diva . . .

JIGGLYPUFF FACTS

- Normal- and Fairy-type Pokémon
- Height: 1'08"
- Weight: 12.1 lbs.
- Evolves into Wigglytuff

Involved with Harry's Disappearance?

Probably not—unless it made Harry fall asleep at the wheel.

MISSING

JIGGLYPUFF

MISSING

LOUDRED

LOUDRED

When Loudred come out to play, they know how to crank up the volume. Loudred is able to shout at crazy levels and uses its ears as loudspeakers to literally knock you down with the beat. It even can temporarily deafen itself! Taking it to eleven is an understatement for these jam masters.

LOUDRED FACTS

- Normal-type Pokémon
- Height: 3'03"
- Weight: 89.3 lbs.
- Evolves into Exploud

Involved with Harry's Disappearance?

Potentially—sound can be more powerful than you might expect.

LUDICOLO

Ludicolo just can't help leaping into a joyful dance when it hears a festive tune.

LUDICOLO FACTS

- Water- and Grass-type Pokémon
- Height: 4'11"
- Weight: 121.3 lbs.
- Evolved form of Lombre

Involved with Harry's Disappearance?

You wouldn't think so, because Ludicolo is so cheerful—but is the cheer covering something up?

MISSING

LUDICOLO

MORELULL

The way Morelull glows in the dark makes its habitat a popular destination for night-time tours—even though it lives in dark, damp, and generally unpleasant places.

Involved with Harry's Disappearance?

Perhaps this little Pokémon could cast some light on the situation?

MORELULL FACTS

- Grass- and Fairy-type Pokémon
- Height: 0'08"
- Weight: 3.3 lbs
- Evolves into Shiinotic

MISSING

MORELULL

MR. MIME

Mr. Mime is silent, and refuses to say a word. It insists on pantomiming *everything* in painstaking detail—whether it's a conversation, a joke, or even just letting someone know they can shove it. While it may be quick with a gesture, it's not as quick with a getaway. It has a habit of pantomiming its actual escape and running in place or hopping onto an imaginary motorcycle. If a chase stays in place, is it even a chase?

MR. MIME FACTS

- Psychic- and Fairy-type Pokémon
- Height: 4'03"
- Weight: 120.1 lbs.
- Evolved form of Mime Jr.

Involved with Harry's Disappearance?

Maybe. Tim and Detective Pikachu ended up interrogating it (though they haven't had a lot of interrogation practice).

Hitting a Wall

The one thing Mimey here is good at is creating invisible walls for defense. You think it's just pantomiming until, *SPLAT!*, you're lying like putty on the floor. Boom. You just got walled.

MISSING

MR. MIME

MISSING

PSYDUCK

PSYDUCK

Poor Psyduck suffers from terrible headaches, which somehow enhance its psychic powers—but it's often too miserable to control those powers. The pain can even be intense enough to make it cry.

PSYDUCK FACTS

- Water-type Pokémon
- Height: 2'07"
- Weight: 43.2 lbs.
- Evolves into Golduck

Baby on Board

Psyduck rides around on Lucy's back like a baby in a carrier. She wants to keep it comforted . . . but it doesn't seem to always work the way she'd like it to.

Involved with Harry's Disappearance?

If it was, and it's been fooling Lucy, Tim, and Detective Pikachu during this whole investigation, that would be the most epic criminal hoodwinking of all time.

SNUBBULL

Snubbull might look scary at first, but it's easy to befriend and has a habit of becoming spoiled easily. It might attempt to drive off a would-be opponent with a growl—but many people find this Pokémon adorable.

SNUBBULL FACTS

- Fairy-type Pokémon
- Height: 2'00"
- Weight: 17.2 lbs.
- Evolves into Granbull
- Lumpy grumpy on the outside, smooth and sweet as caramel on the inside

Involved with Harry's Disappearance?

This Pokémon is actually quite timid and is more prone to getting bullied than taking on an undercover detective! So, probably not . . . but we don't want to underestimate anyone.

MISSING

SNUBBULL

SQUIRTLE

When Squirtle feels like coming out to play, it sticks close to water, where it can spray foamy blasts for splashing in. Its shell helps it cut through the water very quickly, and also offers it protection in battle.

SQUIRTLE FACTS

- Water-type Pokémon
- Height: 1'08"
- Weight: 19.8 lbs.
- Evolves into Wartortle

Involved with Harry's Disappearance?

It may look cute and innocent, but I'm not so sure . . .

Sea Skills

Because its shell is so aerodynamic, Squirtle can swim at high speeds.

TORTERRA

There's enough room on Torterra's enormous back for several small Pokémon to make their nests.

TORTERRA FACTS

- Grass- and Ground-type Pokémon
- Height: 7'03"
- Weight: 683.4 lbs.
- Evolved form of Grotle

Involved with Harry's Disappearance?

Torterra seem to be peaceful, but they are so large, it's hard to know.

CASE CLOSED?

There you have it. All the clues Detective Pikachu has to go on so far. So, what do you think? Can you start piecing together the mystery to figure out what happened to Harry?

This case has already been an emotional rollercoaster!

Actually, any answers or insight you have would be a big help to Detective Pikachu and Tim. They'll keep the search going, too. And if you need Detective Pikachu, you know where to find him: slowly making his way through a pot of coffee at the Hi-Hat Café. Just, please, *don't* scold him for drinking coffee right before bedtime.

And let me tell you something, kid. I have faith in you. I know you have what it takes to be a world-class detective. After all, you learned from Detective Pikachu.

Help out Detective Pikachu and his investigation by making your own notes and observations. Write down anything suspicious—you never know what might be a clue . . .

AND POKÉMON COEXIST

IF YOU LOVE POKÉMON, DON'T MISS THE *SUPER DELUXE ESSENTIAL HANDBOOK*!